The MONSTER WHO LIED

Once upon a time, in a faraway land,

there lived a monster named Jazzy.

Jazzy was a funny and imaginative monster,

but he had a bad habit of telling lies.

Jazzy loved to tell tall tales about his adventures and accomplishments, even though most of them were not true. His friends, the other monsters in the land, knew that Jazzy was not always truthful, but they still enjoyed listening to his stories..

One day, while wandering through the forest,

Jazzy came across a group of animals

who were very upset.

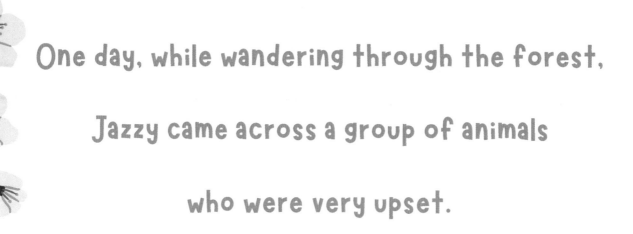

They told him that a big and scary monster

had been stealing their food and frightening them.

They begged Jazzy to help them.

Jazzy saw an opportunity
to impress the animals with a heroic lie about how
he had conquered scary monsters many times.
He promised the animals that he would
defeat the monster and save the day.

The animals were skeptical
but agreed to follow Jazzy.

As they walked deeper into the forest,
Jazzy began to feel nervous.
He had never fought a real monster before,
and he wasn't sure he could do it.

He decided that he had no other option than to lie again...

"Iv'e got this!"

He boasted,

"Iv'e demolished monsters scarier than this in my sleep!"

...That was a lie...

...because inside, he was freaking out...

When they finally reached the dark corner of the forest where the scary monster lived, Jazzy told the animals to go back while he faced the monster alone.

The truth was that Jazzy had no weapon and no plan. He was just hoping that the monster would be scared of him.

But when he saw the monster
Jazzy was the one who got scared.
The monster was

bigger
and
scarier

than he had imagined.

He tried to run away,
but it was too late,
the monster knew he was there!

He tried to think on his feet,
but the only thing that
came to his mind were more lies!

"Don't come near me",
Jazzy exclaimed,
"Laser beams will shoot
from my eyes
and I'll incinerate you!"

...But the scary monster was unfazed. "Go ahead!" He replied, "I can take it!"

Jazzy got nervous.
"Ummm, ummm, ummm,
don't come any closer!
I'll freeze you with my
super-ice-blasting power!"
Jazzy said unconfidently.

The monster, recognizing that Jazzy
was not telling the truth and knowing
the odds were in his favor, replied,
"Go ahead, my heart is
already made of ice – it won't hurt me a bit!"

Jazzy's jig was up

He knew that he couldn't hide
behind his lies anymore
...his stomach began to sink.

"Monster, I lied.
I don't have laser beams
that will incinerate you,
and I can't really
turn you to ice...
but I will tell you the truth.
I am very quick...
Turn around and count to 10,
then try to catch me.
If you can catch me,
you can eat me."

The monster was delighted
at the challenge.

"That's all I have to do?!
This will be an easy meal for me!"
He said as he turned around
and began counting to 10.

Jazzy was quick,
but even more than that,

he was smart.

As the scary monster counted,
Jazzy dug a big hole
and covered it with leaves and sticks.

"8, 9, 10!
Ready or not,
here I come!"

The monster chuckled.

As he ran after Jazzy,
he didn't notice the hole
covered with leaves and sticks,
and fell into it.

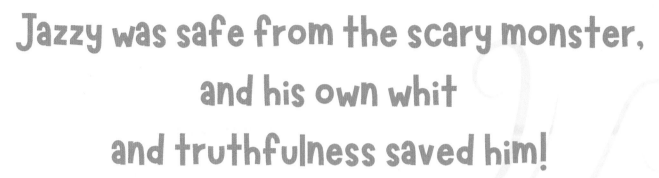

Jazzy was safe from the scary monster,
and his own whit
and truthfulness saved him!

As he walked back to tell his animal friends
the truth about what happened
he realized that telling tall tales never
made his life better, and decided that
he didn't want to lie anymore.

And so,

Jazzy went on to tell the the truth

the rest of his days, knowing that

the truth really will set you free.

Made in the USA
Las Vegas, NV
04 April 2024